the AiRPORT BOOK

by Lisa BROWN

A NEAL PORTER BOOK
ROARING BROOK PRESS
NEW YORK

Copyright © 2016 by Lisa Brown
A Neal Porter Book
Published by Roaring Brook Press
Roaring Brook Press is a division of Holtzbrinck Publishing
Holdings Limited Partnership
175 Fifth Avenue, New York, New York 10010
The art for this book was created using India ink and watercolor
on paper.
mackids.com

Library of Congress Cataloging-in-Publication Data

Names: Brown, Lisa, 1972– author.
Title: The airport book / Lisa Brown.
Description: First edition. | New York : Roaring Brook Press, 2016. | "2016 |
    "A Neal Porter Book." | Audience: Ages 3–7.
Identifiers: LCCN 2015024467 | ISBN 9781626720916 (hardcover)
Subjects: LCSH: Airports—Juvenile literature. | Air travel—Juvenile
    literature.
Classification: LCC TL725.15 .B76 2016 | DDC 387.7/36—dc23
LC record available at http://lccn.loc.gov/2015024467

Our books may be purchased in bulk for promotional, educational, or business use. Please
contact your local bookseller or the Macmillan Corporate and Premium Sales Department
at (800) 221-7945 ext. 5442 or by e-mail at MacmillanSpecialMarkets@macmillan.com.

First edition 2016
Printed in China by Toppan Leefung Printing Ltd., Dongguan City, Guangdong Province
10 9 8 7 6 5

You drive on the highway to where the ground is really flat.

TICKETING CHECK-IN →

LOVE YOU, GRANDMA!

There are lots of people saying lots of goodbyes. Sometimes they hug. Sometimes they cry.

NO PARKING CURB-SIDE DROP OFF

They have big bags on wheels and smaller bags on their shoulders and backs.

Inside the airport you stand in lines.
You stand in lines to get your ticket.
You stand in lines to check your bags.
There are lines for the restrooms.
There are lines to go through security.

A machine x-rays all the bags that you take on the plane.
Sometimes another machine x-rays your body.

You will also take that with you on the plane.

Little sisters cry when they go through the scanner.

You walk past benches and shops and restaurants and art exhibits.
It's like a little indoor town.
Sometimes there are small beeping cars driving through the town.
Sometimes the sidewalks and staircases move by themselves.

You have to hold your little sister's hand tight or she could get lost.

When you reach your gate, you wait. And wait and wait and wait.

Outside, people are getting the plane ready.
They are checking that everything is working and safe and clean and ready to fly.

Things are loaded onto the plane. Gas is put into the fuel tanks. Food is put into the galley. Luggage is put into the cargo hull. The crew put themselves on board and take their places.

Now the passengers can board.
You wait until your group is called
then walk down the jetway.

It looks like an accordion.

You squeeze into your seat.
Some bags go up top.

Some bags go underneath.

You have to make sure that you have all your books and papers
and music and games and toys before the plane takes off.

You listen quietly to the safety announcements. You stow your tray table.

You buckle your seatbelt tight across your lap.

A flight attendant walks up and down the aisle pushing a cart.
Sometimes you get something to drink. Sometimes you get something to eat.

Sometimes there is a movie to watch. Sometimes there are people to talk to.

Sometimes the plane is bouncy, but most of the time it is smooth.

Outside there are clouds and clouds and clouds.

When the plane lands you collect all of your things. You say goodbye to the crew and go to the baggage carousel to find the bags you checked.

You have to make sure that your bag is really *your* bag.

Outside there are lots of people saying lots of hellos.
Sometimes they hug. Sometimes they cry.
Then everyone leaves.

When you leave the airport, you can take a car, a van, a bus, or even a train. We're taking Grandpa's car.

And then you do everything all over again
in the other direction when it's time to go back home.